One Bear at Bedtime

by Mick Inkpen

A Dell Picture Yearling Book

Published by
Dell Publishing
a division of
Bantam Doubleday Dell Publishing Group, Inc.
666 Fifth Avenue
New York, New York 10103

The trademark Yearling® is registered in the
U.S. Patent and Trademark Office.
The trademark Dell® is registered in the
U.S. Patent and Trademark Office.
ISBN: 0-440-40520-3
Reprinted by arrangement with Little, Brown and Company
Printed in the United States of America
October 1991

10 9 8 7 6 5 4 3 2 1

For Simon and Chloë

1

One bear at bedtime
is all I need ...

2

I have two pigs
who wear my clothes . . .

3

Three kangaroos
who bounce on my bed ...

4

Four giraffes
who sit in the bath . . .

5

Five lions who
mess around with
the shampoo ...

6

Six snakes who
unwind the toilet paper…

7

Seven ostriches
who drink my milk . . .

8

Eight crocodiles
who use up all the
toothpaste . . .

9

Nine caterpillars
who crawl about at night...
(Did you spot them?)

10

And a monster
with ten heads
who takes forever
to say good night.

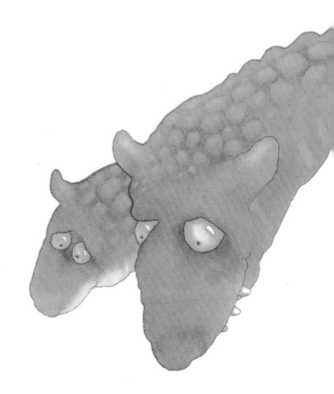

But one bear at bedtime...

...is all I need.